The Athletic SHOE

Other SHOE books by Jeff MacNelly

The Very First SHOE Book
The Other SHOE
The New SHOE
On with the SHOE
A SHOE for All Seasons
The Greatest SHOE on Earth
One SHOE Fits All
Too Old For Summer Camp and Too Young to Retire
A Cigar Means Never Having to Say You're Sorry
Shake *the Hand,* Bite *the Taco*

The Athletic SHOE
Jeff MacNelly

St. Martin's Press   New York

Library of Congress Cataloging-in-Publication Data

MacNelly, Jeff.
  [Shoe. Selections]
  The athletic shoe / Jeff MacNelly.
    p.   cm.
  ISBN 0-312-04873-4
  I. Title.
PS6728.S475M27   1991
741.5'973—dc20   90-28489
                                                                                   CIP

First Edition: October 1991
  10 9 8 7 6 5 4 3 2 1

THERE YOU ARE, THE AGING VETERAN, WONDERING IF YOU STILL HAVE IT.

YOU WONDER IF YOU CAN GET YOUR BODY IN SHAPE FOR YET ANOTHER SUMMER CAMPAIGN.

SO YOU GO TO SPRING TRAINING TO TUNE YOUR BODY, TO HONE YOUR SKILLS, REBUILD YOUR STAMINA ...

TO FIND OUT IF YOU STILL HAVE ENOUGH OF THE OLD MOVES...

TO SEE IF YOU STILL HAVE ONE MORE SEASON LEFT IN YOU...

YUP. LOOKS LIKE I MADE THE CUT AGAIN THIS YEAR...

AND SO, TO RECAP IF I MAY, I'D LIKE SOME FOLLOW-UP FROM YOU ON MY PRIMARY RECOMMENDATIONS...

SO THAT WE CAN START IMPLEMENTING NEAR-TERM STRATEGIC GOALS BY CLOSE OF BUSINESS TODAY.

MY CATCHER RUNS A TIGHT MEETING.

I'LL TRY THE— UMPH!... SLIDER...

FOURTH DOWN!!

I GUESS THIS MEANS THE BASEBALL SEASON IS COMING TO A CLOSE.

AWRIGHT, MEN! HIT THOSE DUMMIES!!.

AAARGH!!

UMPH!

WAIT A SEC... WHO IS THE REAL DUMMY IN THIS PICTURE?

MCNELLY

MEN, I THINK THIS "FRIDGE" THING HAS GOTTEN OUTTA HAND.

I MEAN, WHY DO WE FEEL WE HAVE TO NAME PLAYERS AFTER MAJOR KITCHEN APPLIANCES?...

SHUT UP, TOASTER.

MCNELLY.

Treetops High School was crushed 33-zip last Saturday...

proving once again that, although they're small ...

they're incredibly slow.

TURNOVERS ARE THE KEY TO WINNING FOOTBALL GAMES.

GOOD.

I'LL HAVE TWO MORE OF THE APPLE-CINNAMON.

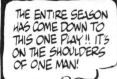

THE ENTIRE SEASON HAS COME DOWN TO THIS ONE PLAY!! IT'S ON THE SHOULDERS OF ONE MAN!

SOMEHOW, HE SENSES THAT THE BLITZ IS ON AS HE TAKES THE SNAP!

COOLY, HE PUTS A MOVE ON THE CHARGING FENCIK"..

AND, SPOTTING A SLIVER OF DAYLIGHT, SPINS OFF RICHARD DENT!!

AND WITH ONE MAN TO BEAT,... STIFF ARMS THE **FRIDGE**!!

AND DASHES IN FOR THE SCORE!!

SKYLER!!

THE BEAUTIFUL MARYBETH DROPS HER MEGAPHONE AND RUNS TO HER HERO!!

THIS IS THE DUMBEST DREAM I HAVE EVER BEEN INVOLVED WITH.

By Jeff MacNelly.

ANY HINTS ON WHICH HORSE I SHOULD BET ON?

YEAH. I HAVE A PERSONAL RULE OF THUMB:

NEVER BET ON A HORSE NAMED AFTER A DOG FOOD.

HOW DO YOU PICK A HORSE ANYWAY?

IT'S EASY.

A LOT OF PEOPLE GET TOO BOGGED DOWN IN STATISTICS. THEY DO RESEARCH, COMPARE TRAINERS, TRACK CONDITIONS, —ALL THAT STUFF. BUT NOT ME.

NO, SIR. I RELY ON THE GOOD OLD GUT REACTION.

I READ THE NAMES OF THE HORSES...

..AND I USUALLY FIND ONE THAT RINGS A BELL—A NAME THAT IS SIGNIFICANT TO ME PERSONALLY.

— HERE, I'LL SHOW YOU. READ OFF THE LINE-UP FOR THE NEXT RACE.

OKAY...

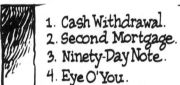

1. Cash Withdrawal.
2. Second Mortgage.
3. Ninety-Day Note.
4. Eye O'You.

5. In the Hole.
6. Chapter Eleven.
7. Belly Up.

HMMM. KIND OF A TOSS-UP SO FAR, ISN'T IT?...

THERE'S ONE PERSON WHO WILL BE CRUCIAL TO YOUR SUCCESS AS A QUARTERBACK...

HE CAN MAKE YOU OR BREAK YOU... HE'S A GUY YOU'LL HAVE TO WORK WITH CLOSELY...

RIGHT, COACH...

I THINK YOU KNOW WHO I'M TALKING ABOUT...

MY SPORTS INFORMATION DIRECTOR?

MEN, AS YOUR PLAYER REP, I WILL BE TAKING OUR DEMANDS TO MANAGEMENT...

NOW, JUST SO WE ARE SURE WE'RE PRESENTING A UNITED FRONT, LET'S GO OVER OUR LIST OF DEMANDS:

NUMBER ONE, I THINK, FOR ALL OF US ON THE J.V. ... IS THE DEMAND THAT THOSE SILLY WATER BOYS AT OUR GAMES BE REPLACED...

WITH WATER GIRLS!!

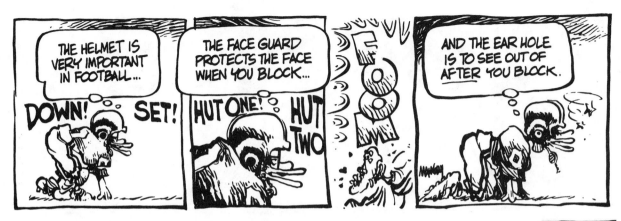

AND SET UP THE GO-AHEAD SCORE FOR THE BAD GUYS...

BUT NOW, IN THE CLOSING SECONDS OF THE GAME ...

I'M CALLED ON TO KICK A FIELD GOAL ...

THIS COULD BE THE CHANCE TO REDEEM MYSELF...

IF THE SNAP IS GOOD, IF THE HOLD IS SOLID,

IF I MAKE IT...

AND IF A FIELD GOAL WERE WORTH 43 POINTS.

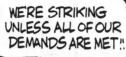

DON'T YOU THINK THEY'RE REACHING A LITTLE WITH THIS PRE-SUPERBOWL SHOW?...

WHAT'S THE MATTER WITH SOME GOOD OL' AMERICAN HYPE?

NO, BOB HOPE IS GREAT... EVEN BROOKE SHIELDS, THE DALLAS CHEERLEADERS AND THE MUPPETS DANCING IN SHOULDER PADS, THAT'S ALL FINE...

BUT THIS... WHAT DOES THIS HAVE TO DO WITH A FOOTBALL GAME?...

JOHN MADDEN TAKING THE TRAIN TO SAN DIEGO IS AN INTEGRAL PART OF THE THRILLING PAGEANTRY THAT IS SUPERBOWL...

MACNELLY

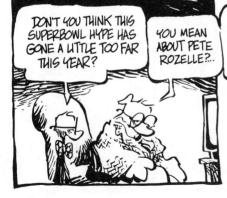

DON'T YOU THINK THIS SUPERBOWL HYPE HAS GONE A LITTLE TOO FAR THIS YEAR?

YOU MEAN ABOUT PETE ROZELLE?...

NO, IF THE COMMISSIONER OF THE NFL WANTS TO BE ON HOLLYWOOD SQUARES, THAT'S OKAY...

BUT THE DAY AFTER THE BIG HAMSTRING PULL TELETHON AND HIS APPEARANCE ON THE JOCK ITCH SEGMENT ON OPRAH?... MORE THAN COINCIDENCE, SEZ I!!...

MACNELLY

BUT WE'RE BETTER THAN OUR RECORD INDICATES.

WE ARE?

SURE.... REMEMBER THE GAME AGAINST MUSHMELON ACADEMY?

THE ONE THAT WAS ALMOST CALLED OFF BECAUSE OF RAIN?

12/10

RIGHT.

IF IT WEREN'T FOR THAT ONE BAD BREAK...

WE'D BE 0 AND 11.

MACNELLY.

Shoe

By Jeff MacNelly

Now for the Hoop Hype, Roundball Roundup, and Dunk Dope...

or Basketball Scores, to the uninitiated.

Milwaukee beat New Jersey, San Antonio beat Denver,

Phoenix beat Houston, Indiana beat Utah, Philadelphia beat Sacramento,

Portland beat New York, Dallas beat Kansas City,

Cleveland beat Detroit, Seattle beat Golden State,

The L.A. Lakers beat the L.A. Clippers, and finally...

an inspired Chicago Bulls team, led by the incomparable Michael Jordan and his 43 points,

totally wiped out, stomped on, and otherwise uglified an out-played, demoralized Boston Celtics squad...

THERE'S NOTHING THAT SAYS SPORTSWRITERS CAN'T BE FANS, TOO.

SKYLER, YOU WANT TO REALLY HELP OUT THIS TEAM?

YOU BET, COACH!

GET IN THERE FOR VALVONI...

RIGHT, COACH!

HEY, VALVONI'S ON THE OTHER TEAM...

THERE'S STILL ROOM IN THIS GREAT GAME OF BASKETBALL FOR THE LITTLE GUY.

SURE. WE MAY NOT BE ABLE TO SLAM DUNK...

BUT WE CONTRIBUTE TO THE TEAM IN OTHER WAYS...

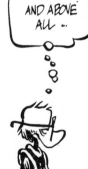

OKAY. IF I MAKE THIS FOUL SHOT WE WIN THE GAME.

I JUST HAVE TO CALM DOWN AND BLOCK OUT THE CROWD NOISE...

MAKE THIS, YOU SPAVIN-LEGGED CANARY ...OR IT'S BENCH CITY FOR YOU!!!

AND ESPECIALLY THE COACH NOISE...

TWEE!!

FOUL?!! ON ME?!

HEY, REF, I NEVER TOUCHED HIM!!

OH.

THAT'S THE FIRST TIME I'VE EVER HEARD OF GETTING CALLED FOR "FOLLOWING TOO CLOSELY."

Jeff MacNelly began drawing SHOE, which appears in more than 1,000 newspapers, in 1977. He won his first Pulitzer Prize in 1972, his second in 1978, and a third in 1985 for his editorial cartoons. He has also won the George Polk Award and twice received the Reuben, the highest honor of The National Cartoonists Society.

A native of Cedarhurst, New York, who attended Phillips Academy, Andover, MacNelly began his career drawing sports and editorial cartoons for his college paper, the *Daily Tar Heel*, at the University of North Carolina. Later, as editorial cartoonist for the town newspaper, *The Chapel Hill Weekly*, MacNelly hit his stride, spoofing the local upheavels and ''ridiculosities'' that characterize North Carolina politics.

His efforts earned the National Newspaper Association's 1969 award for best editorial cartooning, and the following year he became editorial cartoonist for the Richmond, Virginia, *News Leader*. In March 1982, he joined the *Chicago Tribune*.

MacNelly currently resides in Washington, D.C.